NICKI WEISS

Where Does the Brown Bear Go?

PUFFIN BOOKS

PUFFIN BOOKS
Published by the Penguin Group
Penguin Books USA Inc.,
375 Hudson Street, New York, New York 10014, U.S.A.
Penguin Books Ltd, 27 Wrights Lane, London W8 5TZ, England
Penguin Books Australia Ltd, Ringwood, Victoria, Australia
Penguin Books Canada Ltd, 10 Alcorn Avenue, Toronto, Ontario, Canada M4V 3B2
Penguin Books (N.Z.) Ltd, 182-190 Wairau Road, Auckland 10, New Zealand

Penguin Books Ltd, Registered Offices: Harmondsworth, Middlesex, England

First published in the United States of America by Greenwillow Books,
a division of William Morrow & Company, Inc., 1989
Reprinted by arrangement with William Morrow & Company, Inc.
Published in Picture Puffins, 1990
5 7 9 10 8 6 4
Copyright © Monica J. Weiss, 1989
All rights reserved

LIBRARY OF CONGRESS CATALOGING IN PUBLICATION DATA
Weiss, Nicki.   Where does the brown bear go? / Nicki Weiss.   p.   cm.
Summary: When the lights go down on the city streets and the sun sinks far
behind the seas, the animals of the world are on their way home for the night.
ISBN 0-14-054181-0
[1. Animals—Fiction.   2. Night—Fiction]   I. Title.
[PZ7.W448145Wh   1990]   [E]—dc20   89-36027

Printed in Hong Kong
Set in Weidemann Medium

FOR JOHNNY

AND STEVIE

When the lights go down
On the city street,
Where does the white cat go, honey?
Where does the white cat go?

When evening settles
On the jungle heat,
Where does the monkey go, honey?
Where does the monkey go?

They are on their way.

They are on their way home.

When shadows fall
Across the dune,
Where does the camel go, honey?
Where does the camel go?

They are on their way.

They are on their way home.

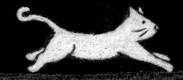

When the sun sinks far
Behind the seas,
Where does the seagull go, honey?
Where does the seagull go?

When night in the forest
Disguises the trees,
Where does the brown bear go, honey?
Where does the brown bear go?

They are on their way.

They are on their way home.

The stars are bright and a warm wind blows
Through the window tonight, honey,
Through the window tonight....

And everyone is home.